The Sky is Falling

Retold by Michèle Dufresne • Illustrations by Michelle Morse

Pioneer Valley Educational Press, Inc.

Bump!

"Oh, no! The sky is falling,"
said Little Chick.
"I will go and tell the king."

"Where are you going?"
said Little Duck.

"The sky is falling,"
said Little Chick.
"I am going to tell the king."

"I will come with you,"
said Little Duck.

"Where are you going?"
said Little Goose.

"The sky is falling,"
said Little Chick.
"I am going
to tell the king."

"I will come with you,"
said Little Goose.

"Where are you going?"
said Little Turkey.

"The sky is falling,"
said Little Chick.
"I am going to tell the king."

"I will come with you,"
said Little Turkey.

"Where are you going?"
said Little Fox.

"The sky is falling,"
said Little Chick.
"I am going to tell the king."

"Oh!" said Little Fox.

"Look down here,"
said Little Fox.

"The king is down here!"

Down went Little Turkey.
"Gobble! Gobble! Gobble!"

Down went Little Goose.
"Honk! Honk! Honk!"

Down went Little Duck.
"Quack! Quack! Quack!"

"Oh, my," said Little Chick.
And she ran and ran
and ran all the way home.

16